"Where is Cuddles?" asked Bob.
"Where is Cuddles?" asked Jan.
"We cannot find Cuddles."

1

2 "Cuddles must be outside," father said.
He went outside to look for Cuddles.
"Cuddles, where are you?"

Father came back inside.
He looked very happy.
"I have a surprise for you!"

3

4

He took Bob and Jan outside.
"Cuddles is under the house," Father said.
"Look under the house."

"Do you see Cuddles?" Father asked.
"Yes, I see Cuddles," said Jan.
"Why is she under the house?" asked Bob.

CHAPTER I

5

6

"Look again," said Father.
"And you will have a surprise."

"Do you see the surprise?" asked Father.
"Yes," said Bob and Jan.
"We see the surprise!"

7

"Cuddles has kittens!" said Jan.
"Cuddles is a mother!" said Bob.
"Oh, that is a good surprise!" said Jan and Bob.

8